Random House 🏠 **New York**

© 2022 Viacom International Inc. All Rights Reserved. Nickelodeon, Santiago of the Seas, and all related titles, logos, and characters are trademarks of Viacom International Inc. Published in the United States by Random House Children's Books, a division of Penguin Random House LLC, 1745 Broadway, New York, NY 10019, and in Canada by Penguin Random House Canada Limited, Toronto. Random House and the colophon are registered trademarks of Penguin Random House LLC.

ISBN 978-0-593-43120-7 (hardcover)

rhcbooks.com

MANUFACTURED IN CHINA

10 9 8 7 6 5 4 3 2 1

SANTIAGO

¡Hola! I'm Santiago, Pirate Protector of Isla Encanto. These are my fellow Pirate Protectors—Lorelai, Tomás, and my coquí frog, Kiko!

We sail the seas aboard *El Bravo,* rescuing friends, finding missing treasure, and spreading kindness. I record all my adventures in my Captain's Journal! This is YOUR Captain's Journal!

Draw yourself in a pirate outfit for your Captain's Journal. Draw your crew, too!

Color *El Bravo!*

I have a lot of cool pirate items
to help me on my adventures!

**CAPTAIN'S
JOURNAL**

EL BRAVO

MAGIC SPYGLASS

MAGIC GAUNTLET

MAGIC SWORD

MAGIC COMPASS

What pirate items do you bring on your adventures? Draw them!

LORELAI

With her bracelet of pearl, Lorelai can change from a mermaid to a girl! Lorelai loves adventures on land and under the sea. And she can use her magic mermaid call to speak to the creatures of the deep! This is Lorelai's octopus pal, Cecilia.

CECILIA

Draw yourself as a merperson!
What underwater friend would you have?

A good pirate needs good spotting skills. Spot the five differences between these two pictures!

See page 65 for all answers.

TOMÁS

TINA

Tomás is my cousin, and the best First Mate ever! He plays Power Chords on his Magic Guitar to create wind, enchant animals, and do other things to help us. Sometimes he gets a little nervous, but he's always there when his pirate pals need him.

Tomás's sister, Tina, *es mi prima*! She's a great inventor. She makes special gadgets that help us on our adventures.

Show Tomás playing a Power Chord by drawing five musical notes!

Draw Tomás's Magic Guitar in the Captain's Journal!
Use the grid to help.

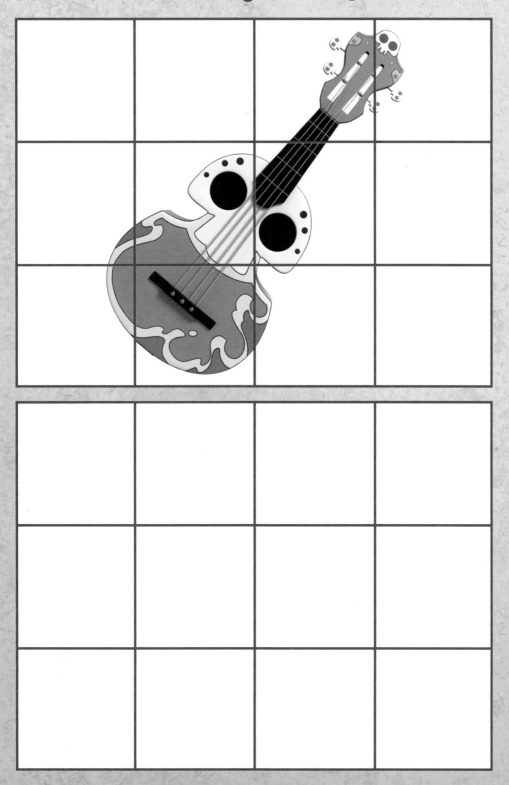

Color the whole crew of
Pirate Protectors, me hearty!

Tina is building inventions to help us protect the seas. Draw an invention you would build.

_____

(your invention's name)

Tomás is my First Mate! Draw someone you'd like to have as your First Mate!

El Bravo is my pirate ship.
Draw your own pirate ship and give it a name.

_____
(your ship's name)

This is my pirate flag.
Draw your own pirate flag.

Match the colors to the objects!

azul

amarillo

morado

rojo

BONNIE BONES

Bonnie wants to be Queen of the Pirates! She wants all the power—and all the pirate booty—for herself. With her Kitty Cat Crew and her crow sidekick, Sir Butterscotch, she's always causing trouble!

SIR BUTTERSCOTCH

KITTY CAT CREW

ENRIQUE RÉAL DE PALACIOS THE THIRD

This greedy pirate always wants the best and the fanciest things . . . no matter who they belong to. He has his *ratoncitos* do all the work for him aboard his ship, *El Palacio,* because he likes to keep his coat clean!

RATONCITOS

ESCARLATA LA PIRATA

Part jellyfish, part girl, and all trouble, Escarlata wants to rule the seas. She lives in a sunken ship, where she mixes magic potions and commands an army of jellyfish!

Match the bad pirates to their sidekicks!

TIME FOR ADVENTURE!

The Captain's Journal holds the legends, myths, and treasures of Isla Encanto and beyond! Help me and my crew complete our pirate adventures and record them in your journal for future Pirate Protectors!

THE LEGEND OF CAPITÁN CALAVERA

Capitán Calavera was the first Pirate Protector of Isla Encanto. He sailed the High Seas on *El Bravo* and used his Magic Compass, El Corazón de Oro, to find his way. When Santiago found his compass, he became the island's new Pirate Protector!

Show us the way to the treasure so we can return it to the people of Isla Encanto!

START

FINISH

Whenever we set sail on an adventure, our pirate outfits magically appear on us.

Color my pirate outfit.

Tomás aims to be the best First Mate ever!
Which picture below matches the top one?

THE STORY OF THE LUCKY STAR

The Lucky Star was the most priceless treasure of Isla Encanto. It brought good luck to all on the island. But one night it was stolen by the bad pirate José Jones. His ship and the Lucky Star sank in a storm, and haven't been seen since. Santiago needed to retrieve it!

Which path should Lorelai and I take to find the Lucky Star?

A
B
C

35

CAPITÁN ESPECTRO

Legend has it that Capitán Espectro abandoned his ghost ship to save his crew, and he's been looking for it ever since. When he took his ghost ship back, Cecilia, who had been hiding, went along with it!

Cecilia is hidden on
the ghost ship.
Do you see her?

THE GOLDEN GIANT

Long ago, the villagers of the island put their gold into a lake, El Lago de Oro, and protected it with a spell. If even a single piece was taken, it would awaken a Golden Giant. And this giant would not rest until every last piece of gold was back in the lake.

Enrique stole four pieces of gold!
Draw some gold to give back to the Golden Giant.

THE STONE OF LIFE

La Piedra de la Vida is an ancient jewel with mysterious magical powers. Legend says it was lost a long time ago on an uncharted island. Though many have searched for it, it has never been found.

Color the missing part of the map to lead the Pirate Protectors to La Piedra de la Vida!

THE TREASURE OF *EL BRAVO*

One day, Santiago and his pirate crew discovered something glowing beneath the floorboards of *El Bravo*. It was El Corazón Dorado, the Golden Heart. According to legend, it was one of the most powerful treasures in the Seven Seas! The Golden Heart's energy gave *El Bravo* its superpowers!

Enrique stole the heart, but Santiago knew who could help: his *prima* Tina! She had a great invention that could help Santiago catch Enrique in his underwater vehicle.

Circle the invention that would help the crew sail the seas again!

Which path will lead
the cousins to Enrique?

A B C

If the heart got wet, its power would stop. Enrique got it wet, but a good pirate never gives up!

Help Santiago make the heart work again by coloring it. Use lots of bright colors!

THE MAGIC PIRATE

Magic is everywhere, but the best magician in the Seven Seas is the Magic Pirate. He lives on La Isla Mágica in a magical castle. Legend says the island is full of menacing magic, so you have to be extra brave to visit!

Use the key to color the picture and make the castle stage magically appear!

KEY

1 = red   2 = blue   3 = gold

TRITON'S TRUMPET

Kept under the sea in a treasure chest that can only be opened by a mermaid's song is Triton's Trumpet. If you blow on it, you can control the water and make it do whatever you want!

Draw a big wave to carry *El Bravo*!

THE CURSE OF THE PIRATE BABY

A long time ago, a young prince hid his favorite treasures deep in a lake. He cast a spell to protect them so that anyone who touched the enchanted water would be turned into a baby. According to legend, the pirate who finds the treasure will break the curse—so they keep trying. But each one has turned into a baby!

When Bonnie tried to steal the treasure, she turned into a baby. Baby Bonnie wants treasure!

Draw a treasure that a baby would love.

LA CAVERNA SECRETA

Mami Josefina found a painting of a famous island chief, his legendary treasure, and his medallion, made of rare ruby gold. According to a map, he hid his treasure and his medallion somewhere in La Caverna Secreta.

Follow the path to find the treasure!

START

FINISH

THE DIAMOND SKULL

One of the legendary treasures that Capitán Calavera never found was the colorful, sparkling Diamond Skull. It was said to be at the top of a big mountain, and the pirate who found it would see it sparkle!

Color the Diamond Skull, then add its sparkles!

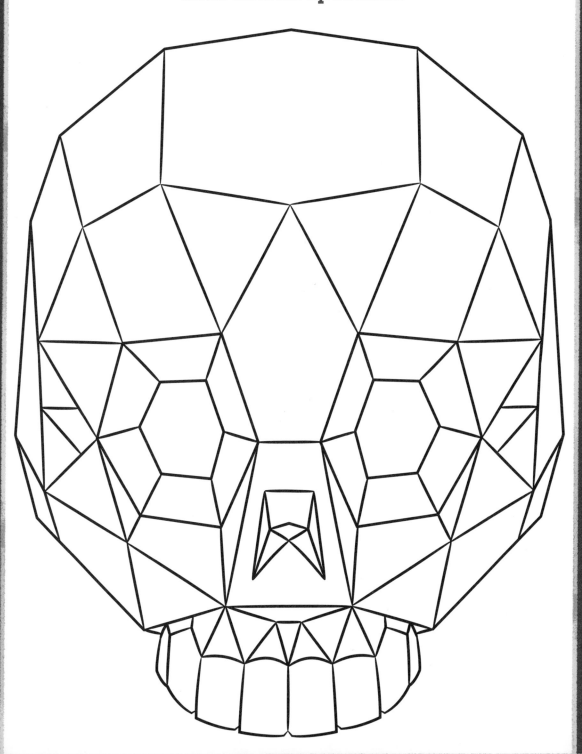

Swashbuckler Squares!

Take turns with a pirate friend drawing a line to connect two dots. If you complete a box, write your initials in it and take another turn. Each player gets one point for each regular box and two points for each box containing one of Santiago's special tools. At the end of the game, the player with more points wins!

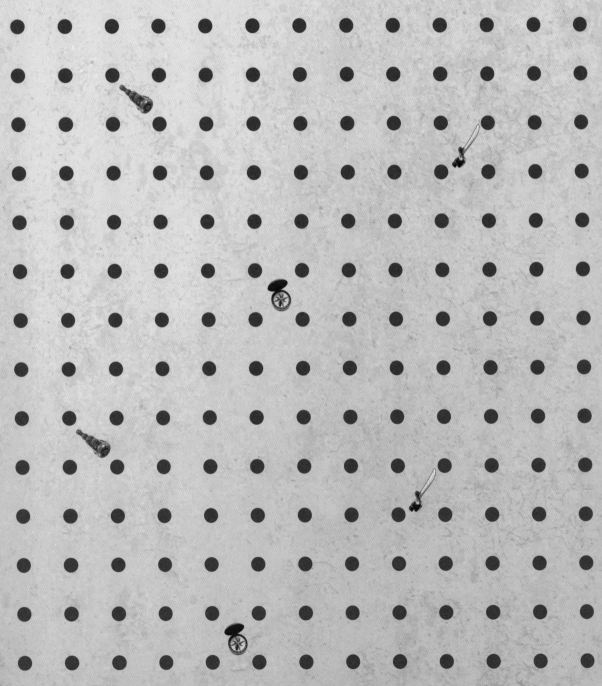

Play again!

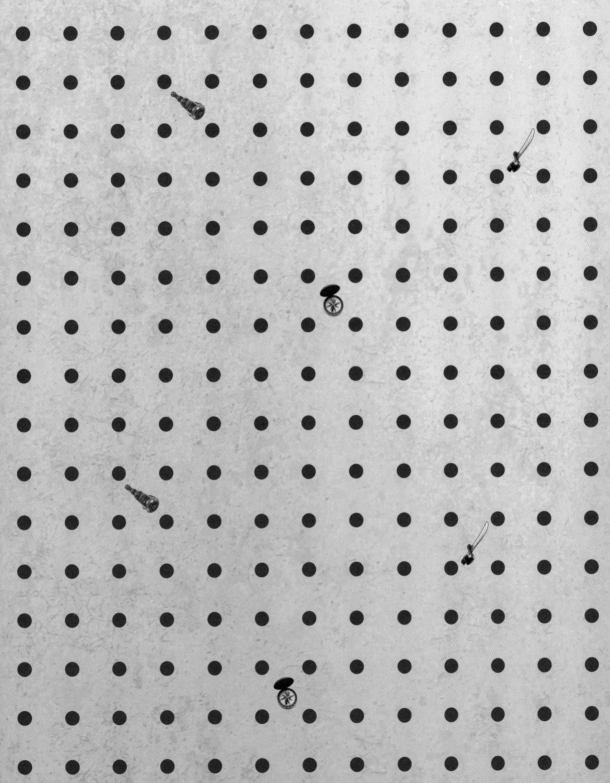

My Magic Spyglass can make things appear extra big! Match all the Pirate Protectors to their close-ups.

Spot the five differences between these two pictures.

What is Lorelai looking at?
Draw it here!

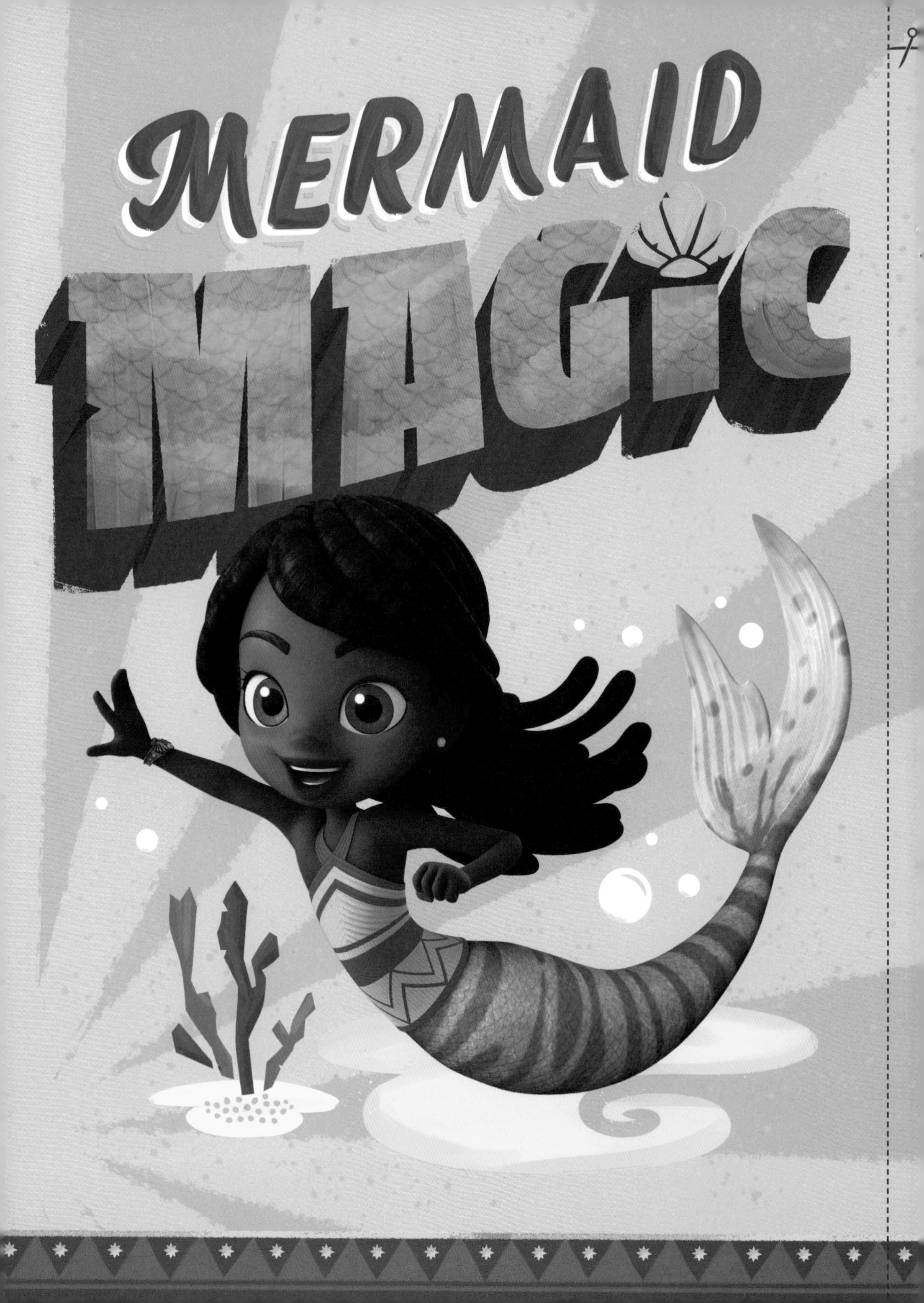
MERMAID
MAGIC